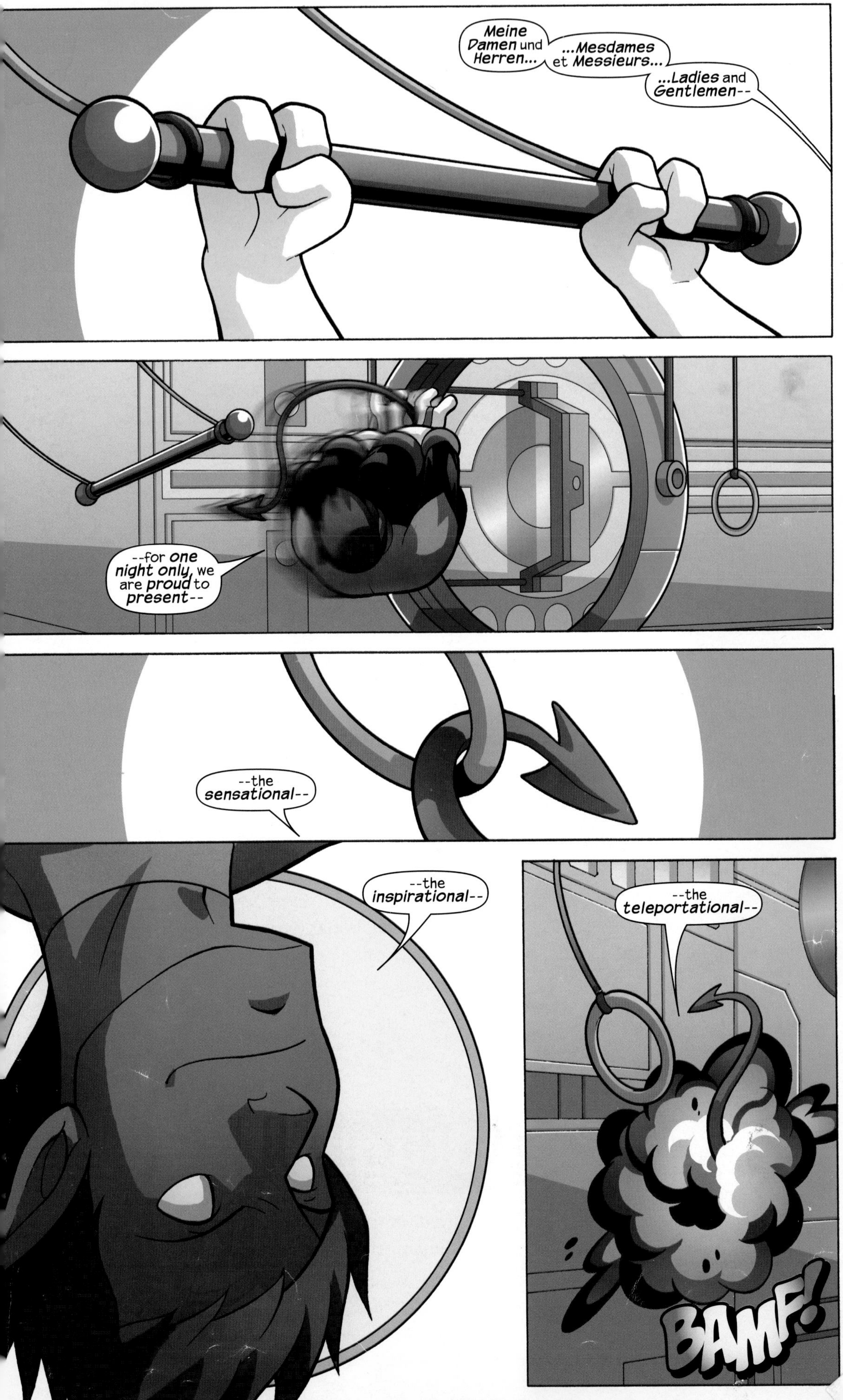
Meine Damen und Herren...
...Mesdames et Messieurs...
...Ladies and Gentlemen--
--for one night only, we are proud to present--
--the sensational--
--the inspirational--
--the teleportational--
BAMF!

VISIT US AT
www.abdopublishing.com

Cataloging Data

Sumerak, Marc
  Big trouble at the big top! / Marc Sumerak, writer ; GuriHiru, art ; Dave Sharpe, letters. -- Library bound ed.
      p. cm. -- (X-Men power pack)
   Summary: Marvel's youngest superheroes Alex, Julie, Jack, and Katie team up with their idols Wolverine, Cyclops, and the other X-Men to keep the world a safer place.
   "Marvel age"--Cover.
   Revision of the February 2006 issue of Marvel age X-Men Power Pack.
   ISBN-13: 978-1-59961-219-5
   ISBN-10: 1-59961-219-4
   1. Superheroes (Fictitious characters)--Comic books, strips, etc.--Fiction.
   2. Graphic novels. I. Title. II. Series.

741.5dc22

All Spotlight books are reinforced library binding
and manufactured in the United States of America

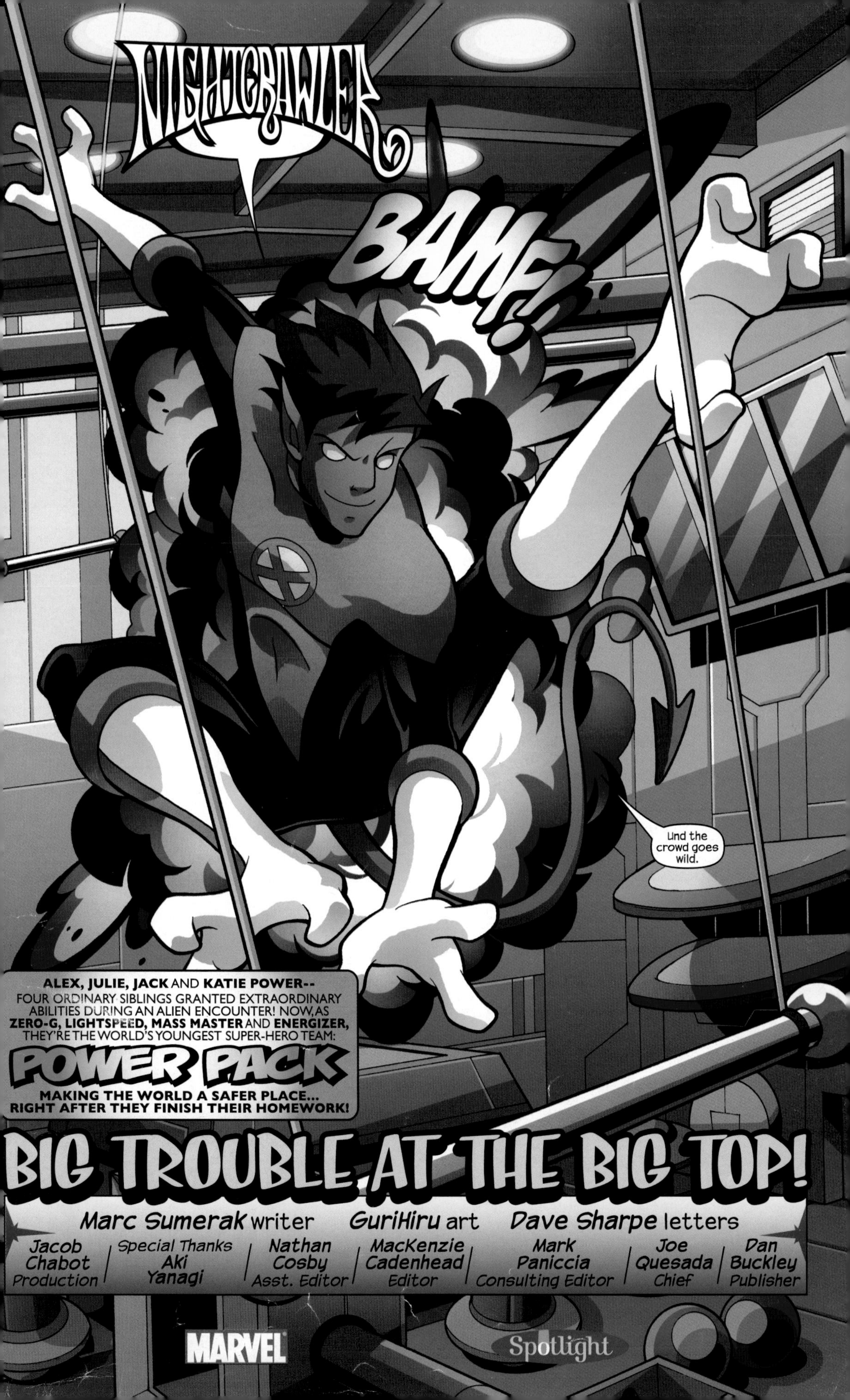
NIGHTCRAWLER
BAMF!!
Und the crowd goes wild.
ALEX, JULIE, JACK AND KATIE POWER-- FOUR ORDINARY SIBLINGS GRANTED EXTRAORDINARY ABILITIES DURING AN ALIEN ENCOUNTER! NOW, AS ZERO-G, LIGHTSPEED, MASS MASTER AND ENERGIZER, THEY'RE THE WORLD'S YOUNGEST SUPER-HERO TEAM:
POWER PACK
MAKING THE WORLD A SAFER PLACE... RIGHT AFTER THEY FINISH THEIR HOMEWORK!
BIG TROUBLE AT THE BIG TOP!
Marc Sumerak writer GuriHiru art Dave Sharpe letters
Jacob Chabot Production | Special Thanks Aki Yanagi | Nathan Cosby Asst. Editor | MacKenzie Cadenhead Editor | Mark Paniccia Consulting Editor | Joe Quesada Chief | Dan Buckley Publisher
MARVEL
Spotlight

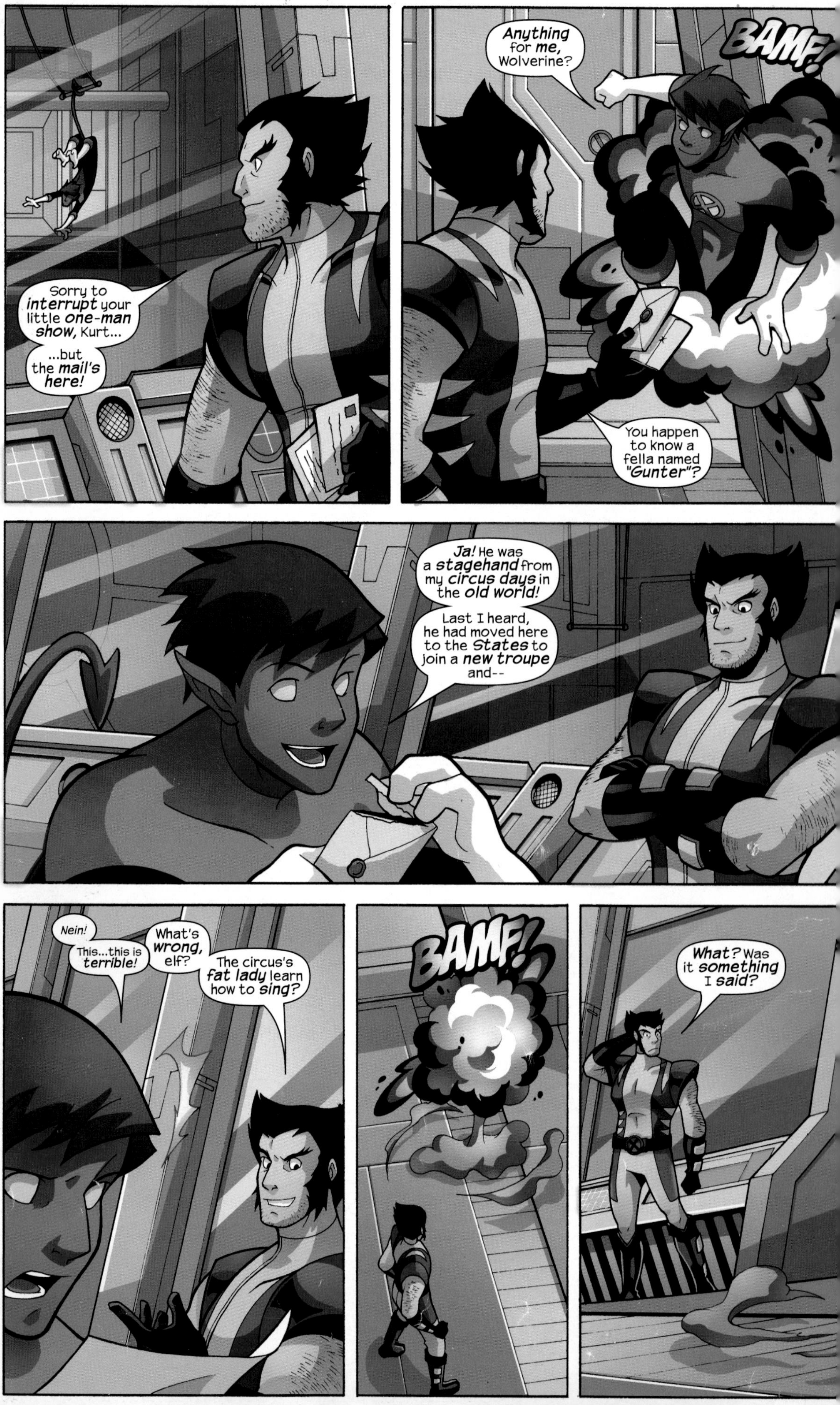
Sorry to interrupt your little one-man show, Kurt...
...but the mail's here!
BAMF!
Anything for me, Wolverine?
You happen to know a fella named "Gunter"?
Ja! He was a stagehand from my circus days in the old world!
Last I heard, he had moved here to the States to join a new troupe and--
Nein!
This...this is terrible!
What's wrong, elf?
The circus's fat lady learn how to sing?
BAMF!
What? Was it something I said?

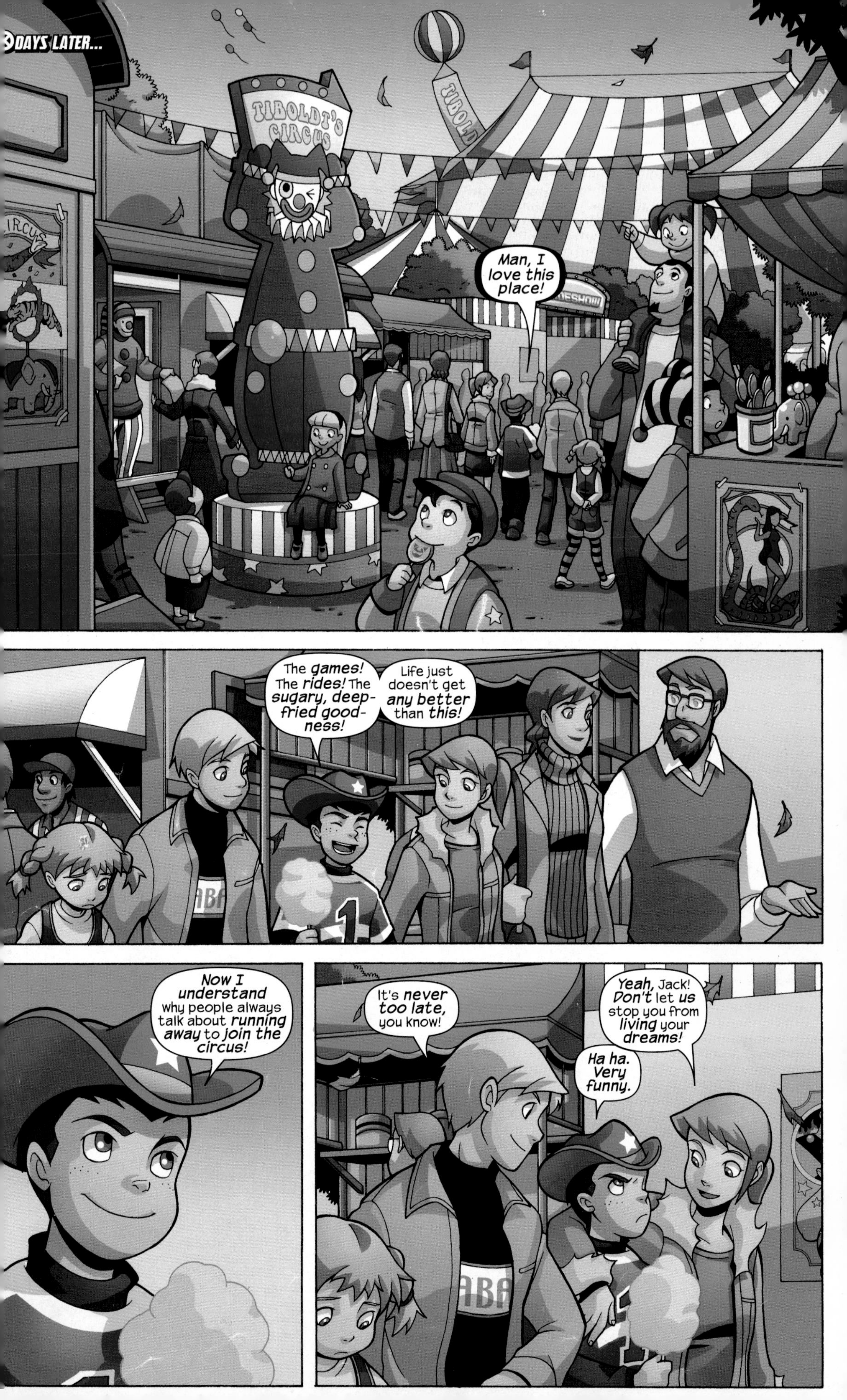
DAYS LATER...
TIBOLDI'S CIRCUS
Man, I love this place!
The games! The rides! The sugary, deep-fried good-ness!
Life just doesn't get any better than this!
Now I understand why people always talk about running away to join the circus!
It's never too late, you know!
Yeah, Jack! Don't let us stop you from living your dreams!
Ha ha. Very funny.

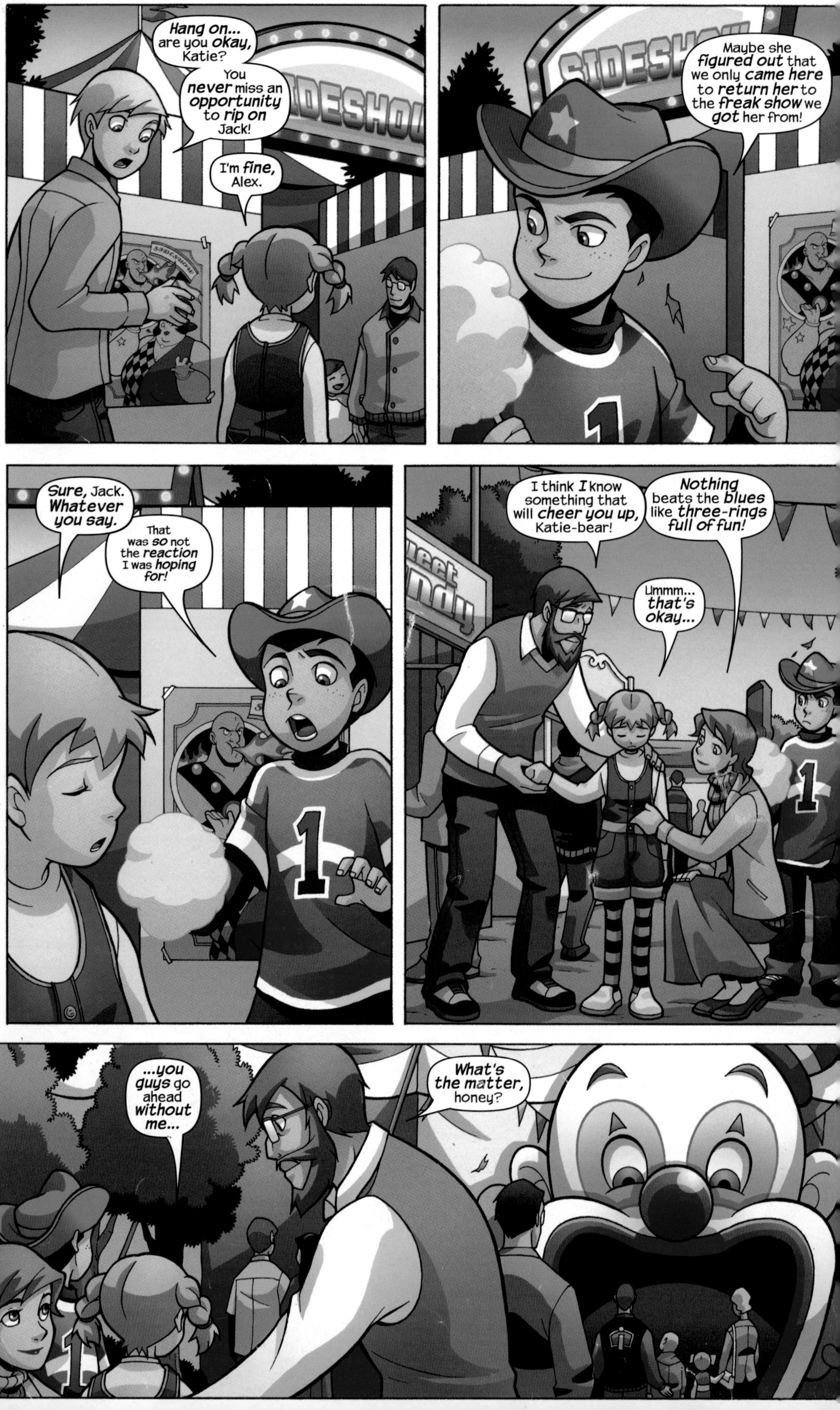
Hang on... are you okay, Katie?
You never miss an opportunity to rip on Jack!
SIDESHOW
I'm fine, Alex.
Maybe she figured out that we only came here to return her to the freak show we got her from!
Sure, Jack. Whatever you say.
That was so not the reaction I was hoping for!
I think I know something that will cheer you up, Katie-bear!
Nothing beats the blues like three-rings full of fun!
Ummm... that's okay...
...you guys go ahead without me...
What's the matter, honey?

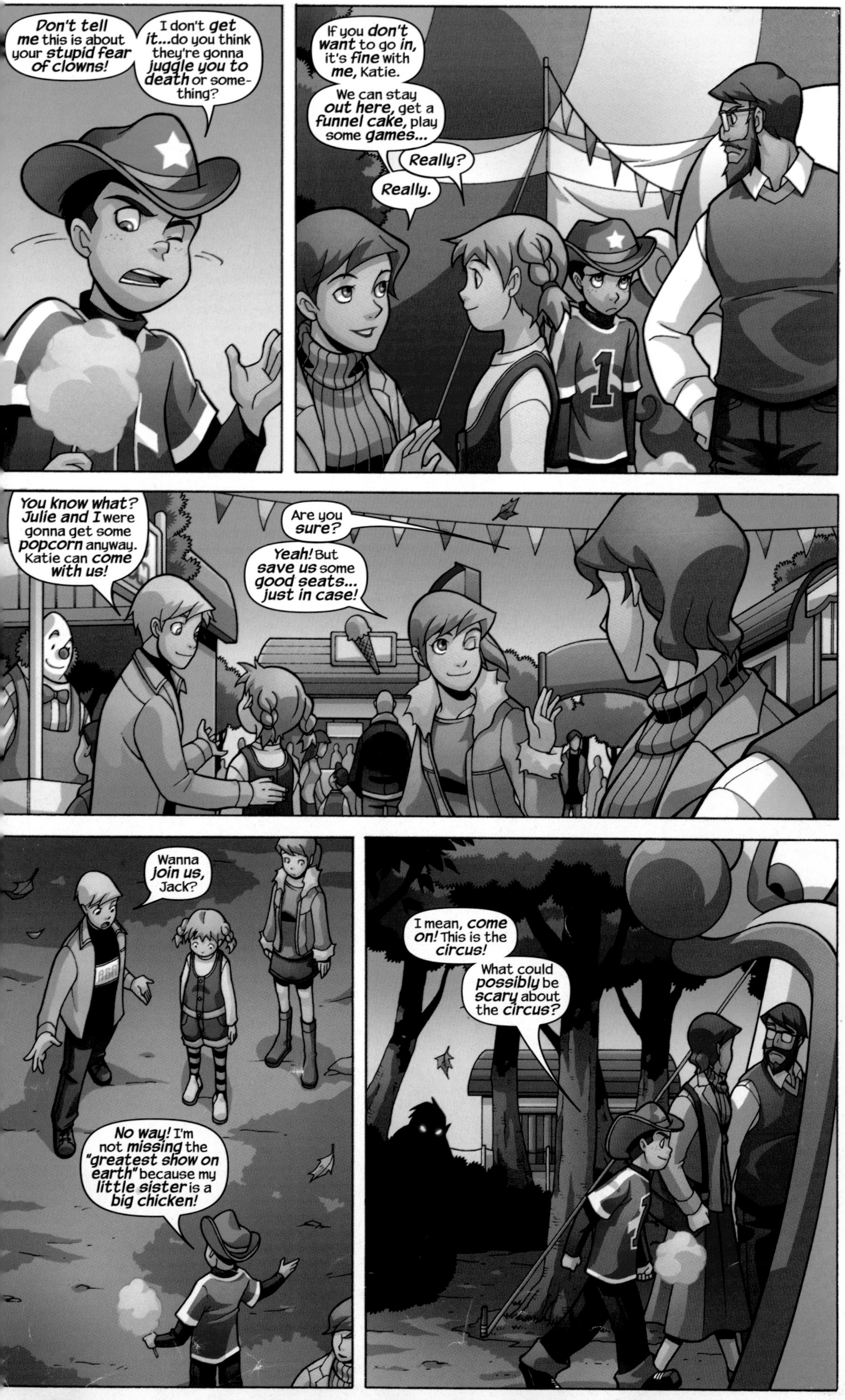
Don't tell me this is about your stupid fear of clowns!
I don't get it...do you think they're gonna juggle you to death or something?
If you don't want to go in, it's fine with me, Katie.
We can stay out here, get a funnel cake, play some games...
Really?
Really.
You know what? Julie and I were gonna get some popcorn anyway. Katie can come with us!
Are you sure?
Yeah! But save us some good seats... just in case!
Wanna join us, Jack?
No way! I'm not missing the "greatest show on earth" because my little sister is a big chicken!
I mean, come on! This is the circus!
What could possibly be scary about the circus?

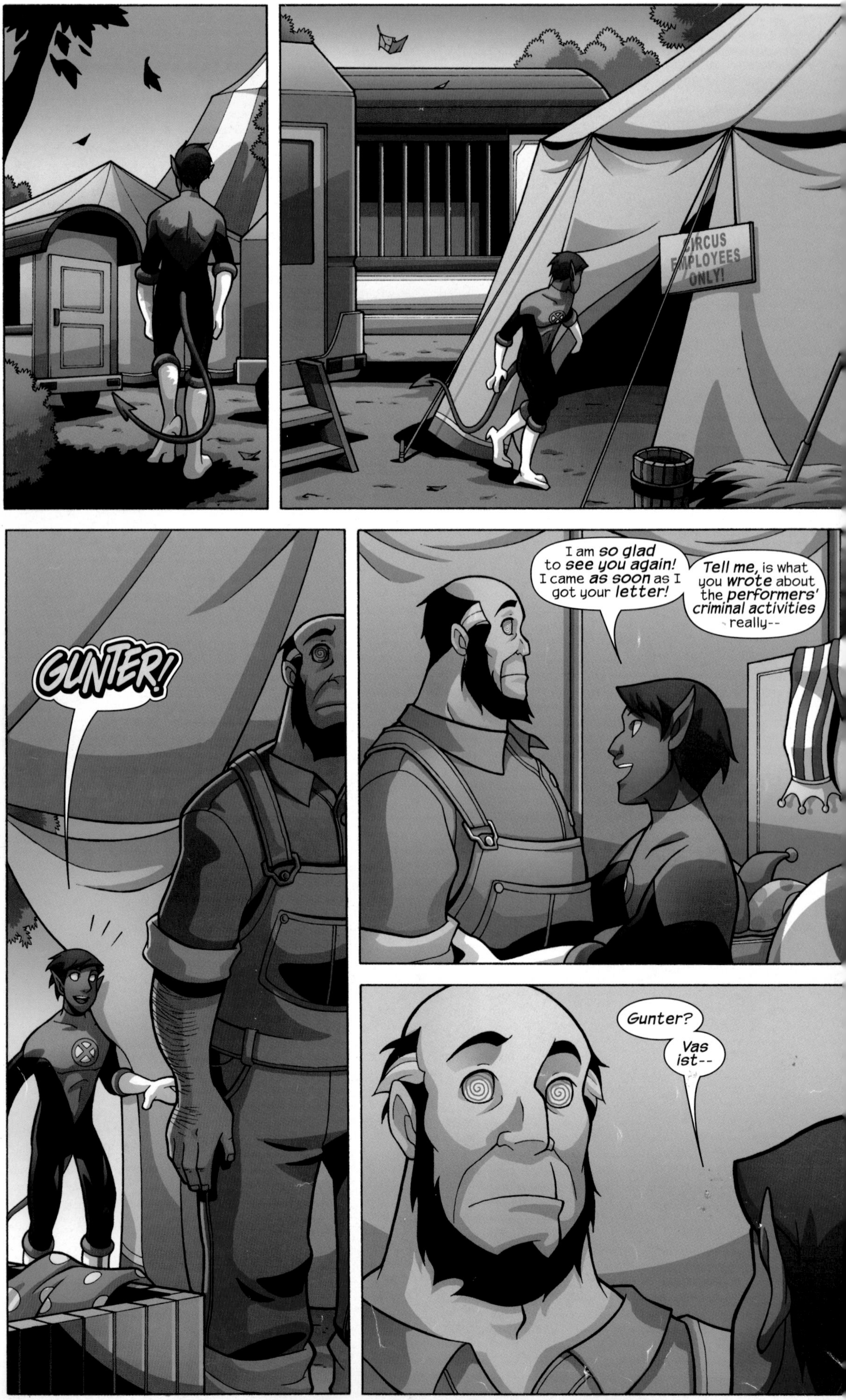
CIRCUS EMPLOYEES ONLY!
GUNTER!
I am *so glad* to *see you again!* I came *as soon* as I got your *letter!*
Tell me, is what you *wrote* about the *performers' criminal activities* really--
Gunter?
Vas ist--

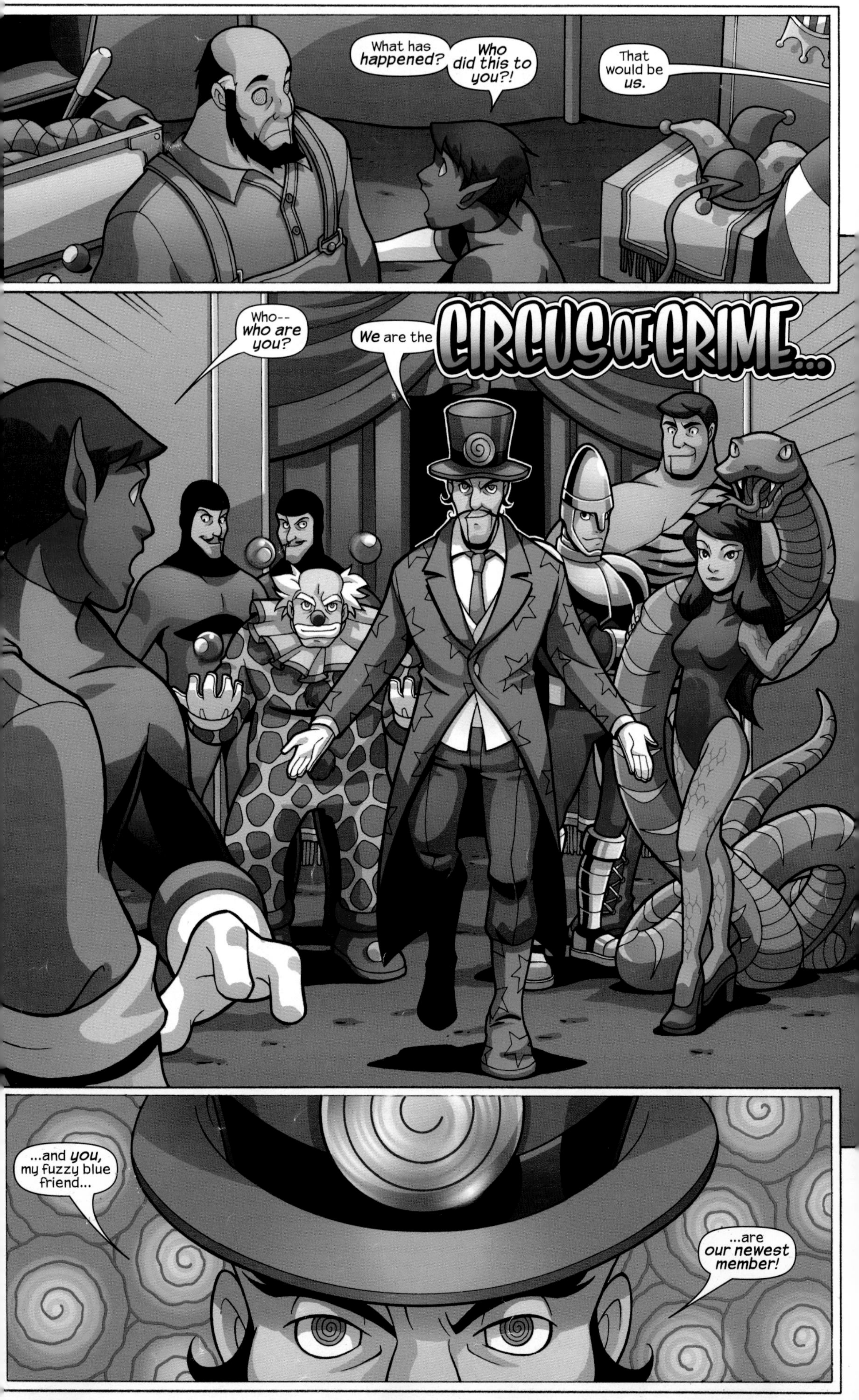
What has happened?
Who did this to you?!
That would be us.
Who-- who are you?
We are the CIRCUS OF CRIME...
...and you, my fuzzy blue friend...
...are our newest member!

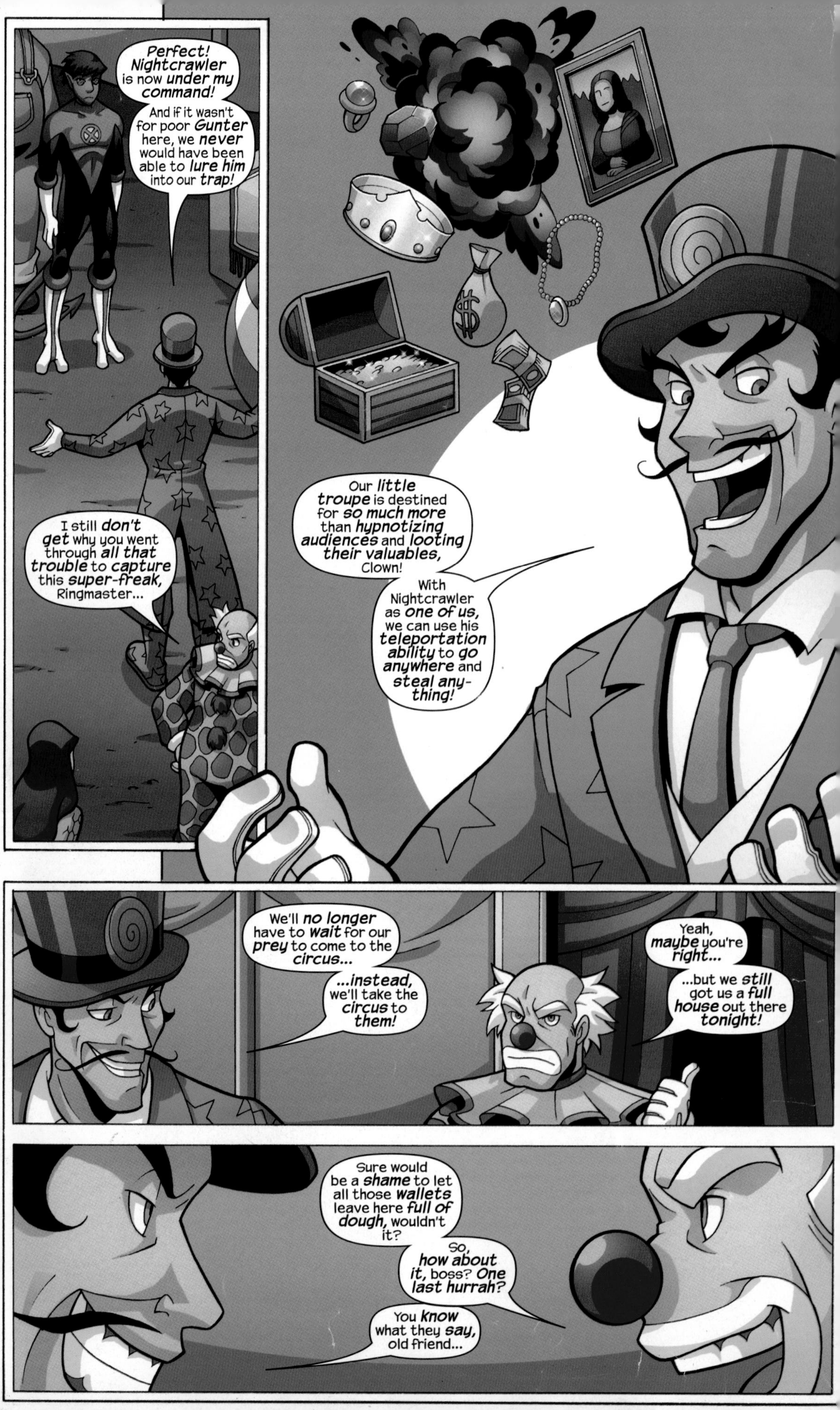

Perfect! Nightcrawler is now under my command!
And if it wasn't for poor Gunter here, we never would have been able to lure him into our trap!
I still don't get why you went through all that trouble to capture this super-freak, Ringmaster...
Our little troupe is destined for so much more than hypnotizing audiences and looting their valuables, Clown!
With Nightcrawler as one of us, we can use his teleportation ability to go anywhere and steal any-thing!
We'll no longer have to wait for our prey to come to the circus...
...instead, we'll take the circus to them!
Yeah, maybe you're right...
...but we still got us a full house out there tonight!
Sure would be a shame to let all those wallets leave here full of dough, wouldn't it?
So, how about it, boss? One last hurrah?
You know what they say, old friend...

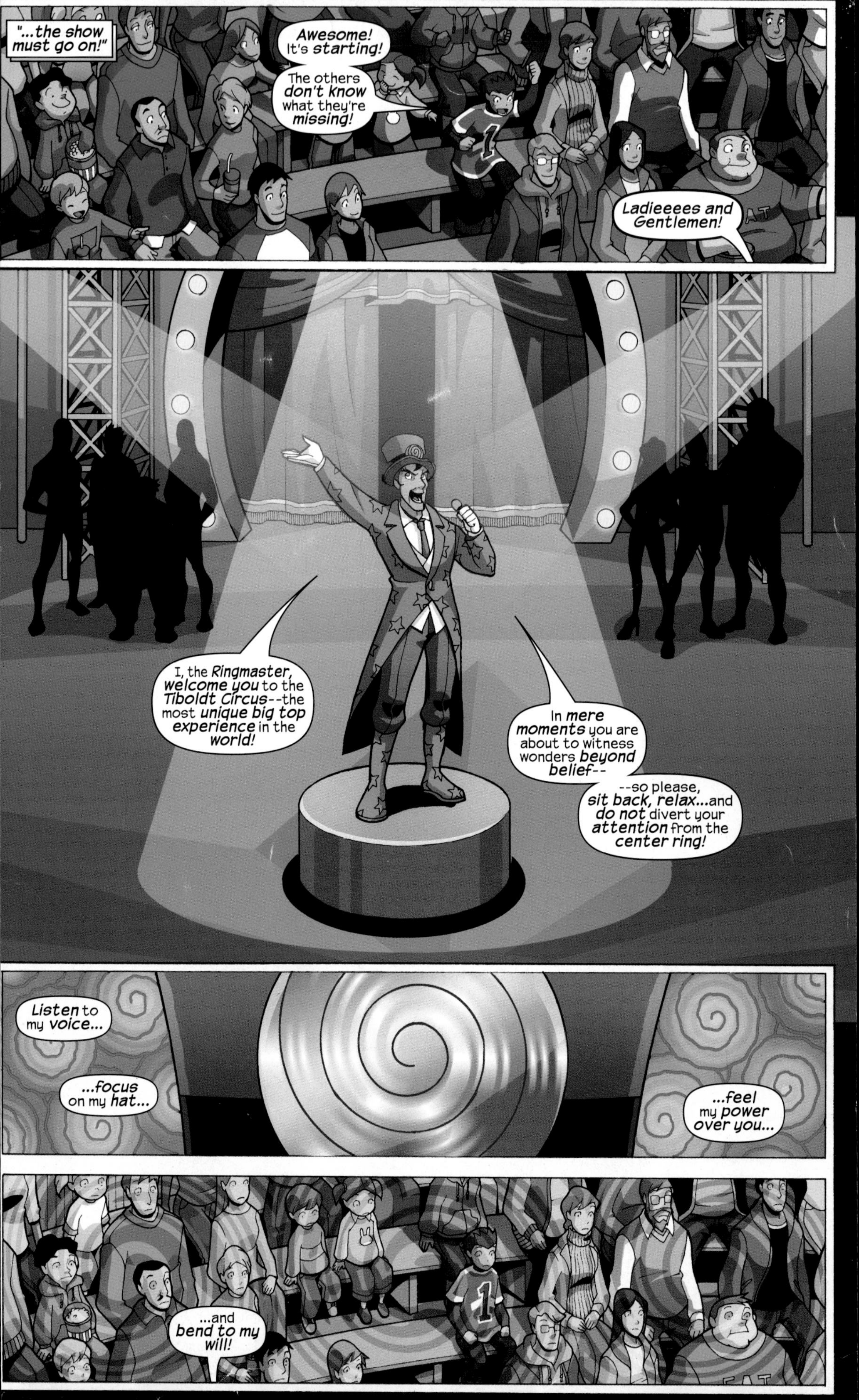
"...the show must go on!"
Awesome! It's starting!
The others don't know what they're missing!
Ladieeees and Gentlemen!
I, the Ringmaster, welcome you to the Tiboldt Circus--the most unique big top experience in the world!
In mere moments you are about to witness wonders beyond belief--
--so please, sit back, relax...and do not divert your attention from the center ring!
Listen to my voice...
...focus on my hat...
...feel my power over you...
...and bend to my will!

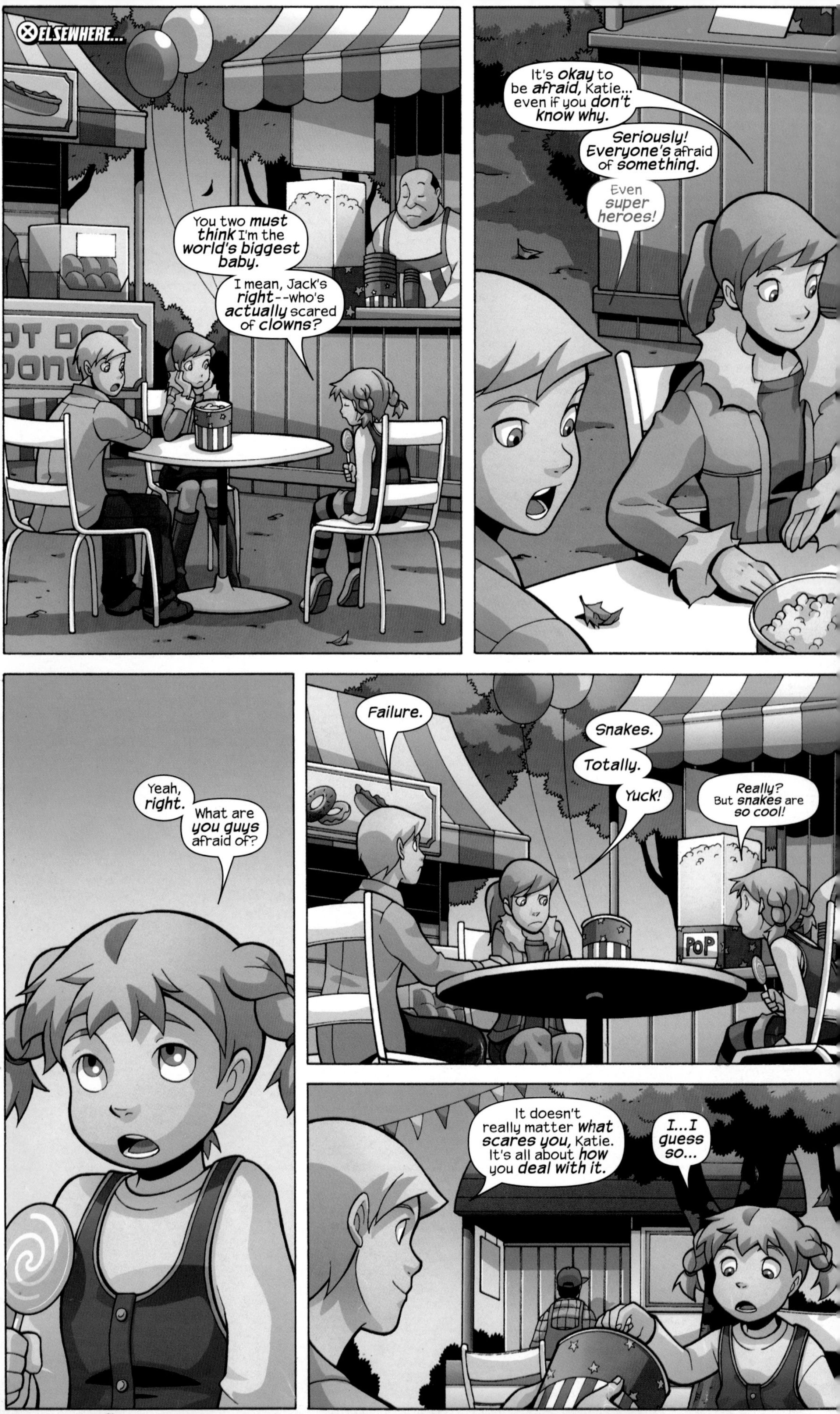
ELSEWHERE...
You two must think I'm the world's biggest baby.
I mean, Jack's right--who's actually scared of clowns?
It's okay to be afraid, Katie... even if you don't know why.
Seriously! Everyone's afraid of something.
Even super heroes!
Yeah, right.
What are you guys afraid of?
Failure.
Snakes.
Totally.
Yuck!
Really? But snakes are so cool!
PoP
It doesn't really matter what scares you, Katie. It's all about how you deal with it.
I...I guess so...

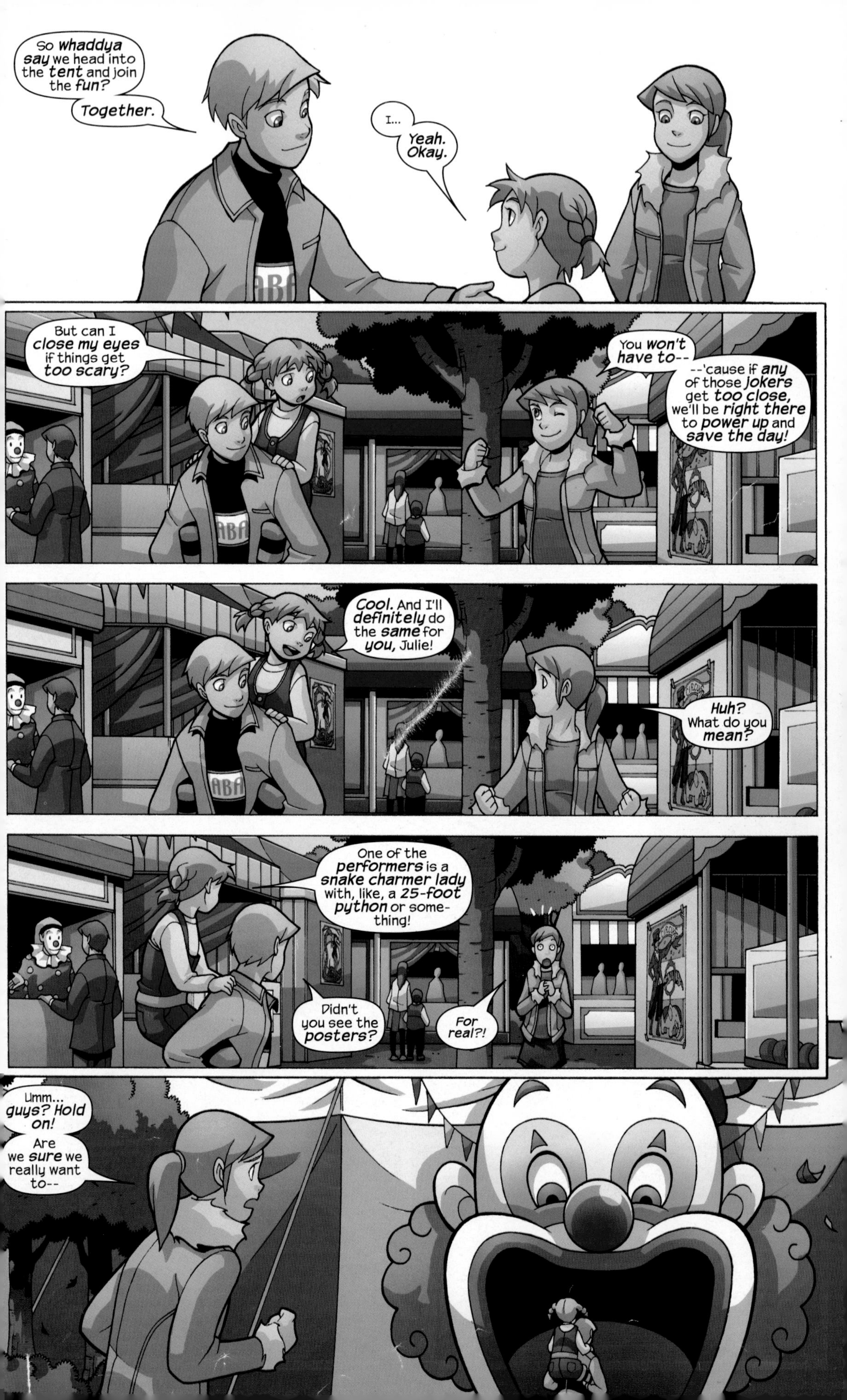
So whaddya say we head into the tent and join the fun?
Together.
I...
Yeah. Okay.
But can I close my eyes if things get too scary?
You won't have to--
--'cause if any of those jokers get too close, we'll be right there to power up and save the day!
Cool. And I'll definitely do the same for you, Julie!
Huh? What do you mean?
One of the performers is a snake charmer lady with, like, a 25-foot python or some-thing!
Didn't you see the posters?
For real?!
Umm... guys? Hold on!
Are we sure we really want to--

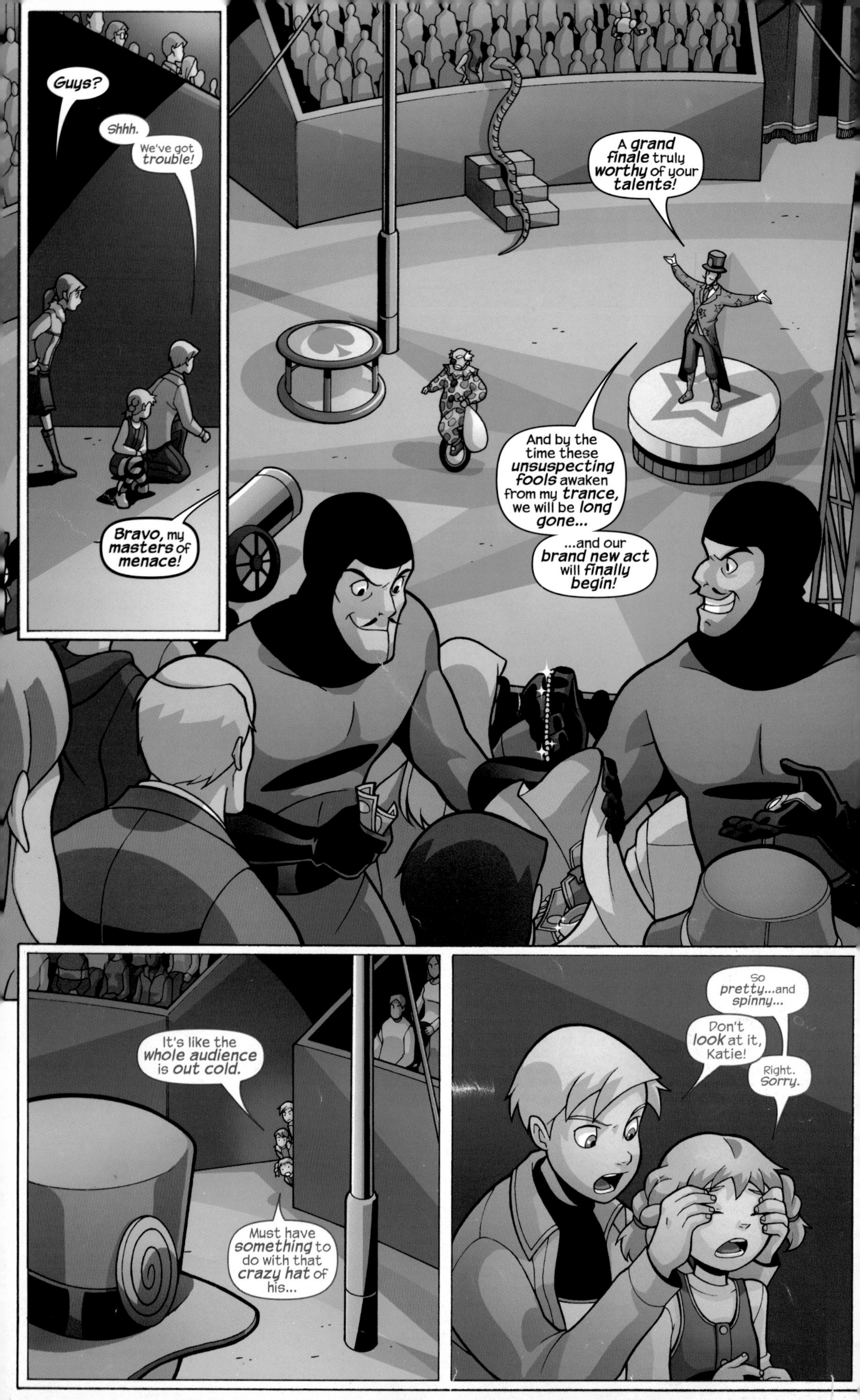
Guys?
Shhh.
We've got trouble!
Bravo, my masters of menace!
A grand finale truly worthy of your talents!
And by the time these unsuspecting fools awaken from my trance, we will be long gone...
...and our brand new act will finally begin!
It's like the whole audience is out cold.
Must have something to do with that crazy hat of his...
So pretty...and spinny...
Don't look at it, Katie!
Right. Sorry.

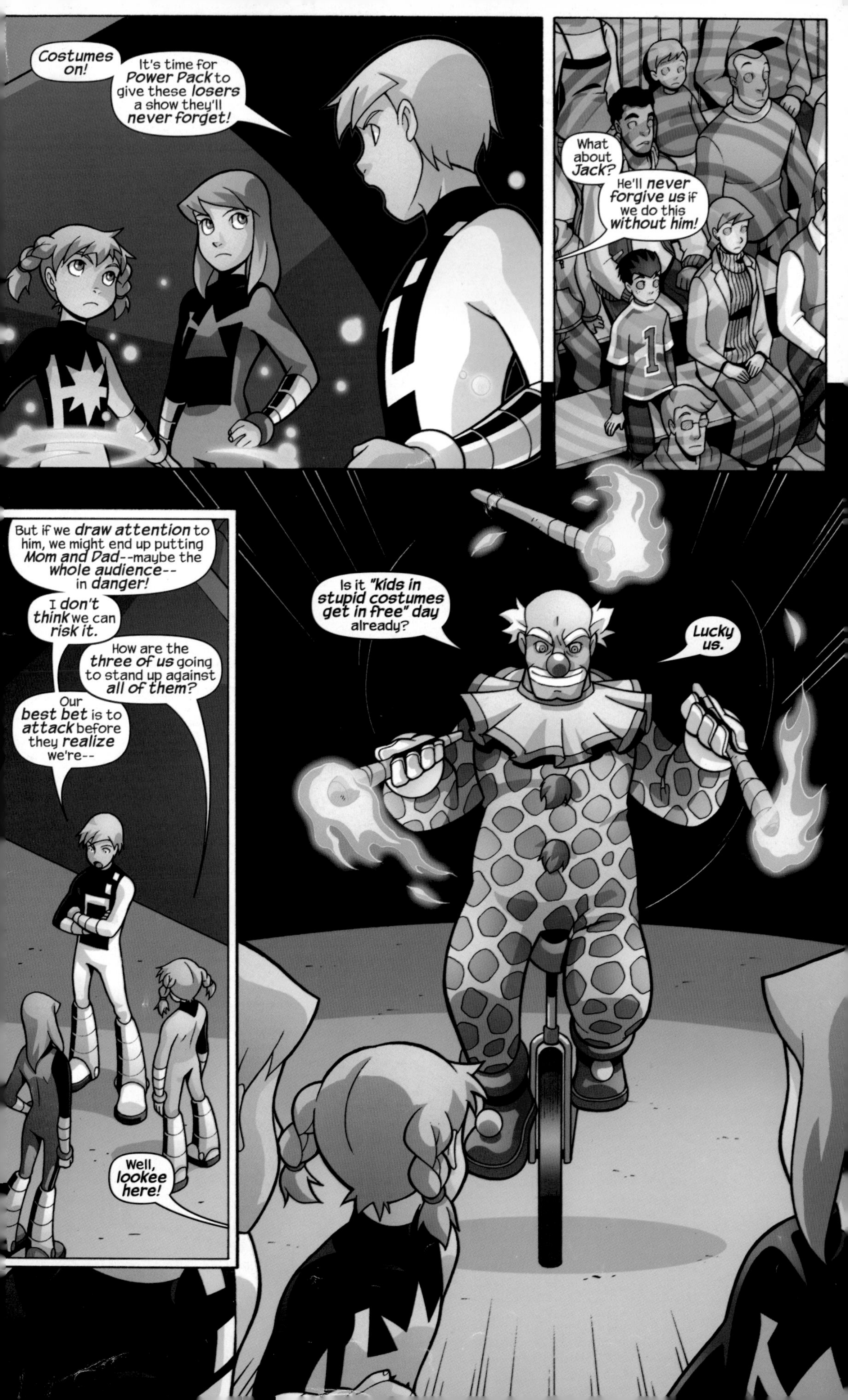
Costumes on!
It's time for Power Pack to give these losers a show they'll never forget!
What about Jack?
He'll never forgive us if we do this without him!
But if we draw attention to him, we might end up putting Mom and Dad--maybe the whole audience--in danger!
I don't think we can risk it.
How are the three of us going to stand up against all of them?
Our best bet is to attack before they realize we're--
Well, lookee here!
Is it "kids in stupid costumes get in free" day already?
Lucky us.

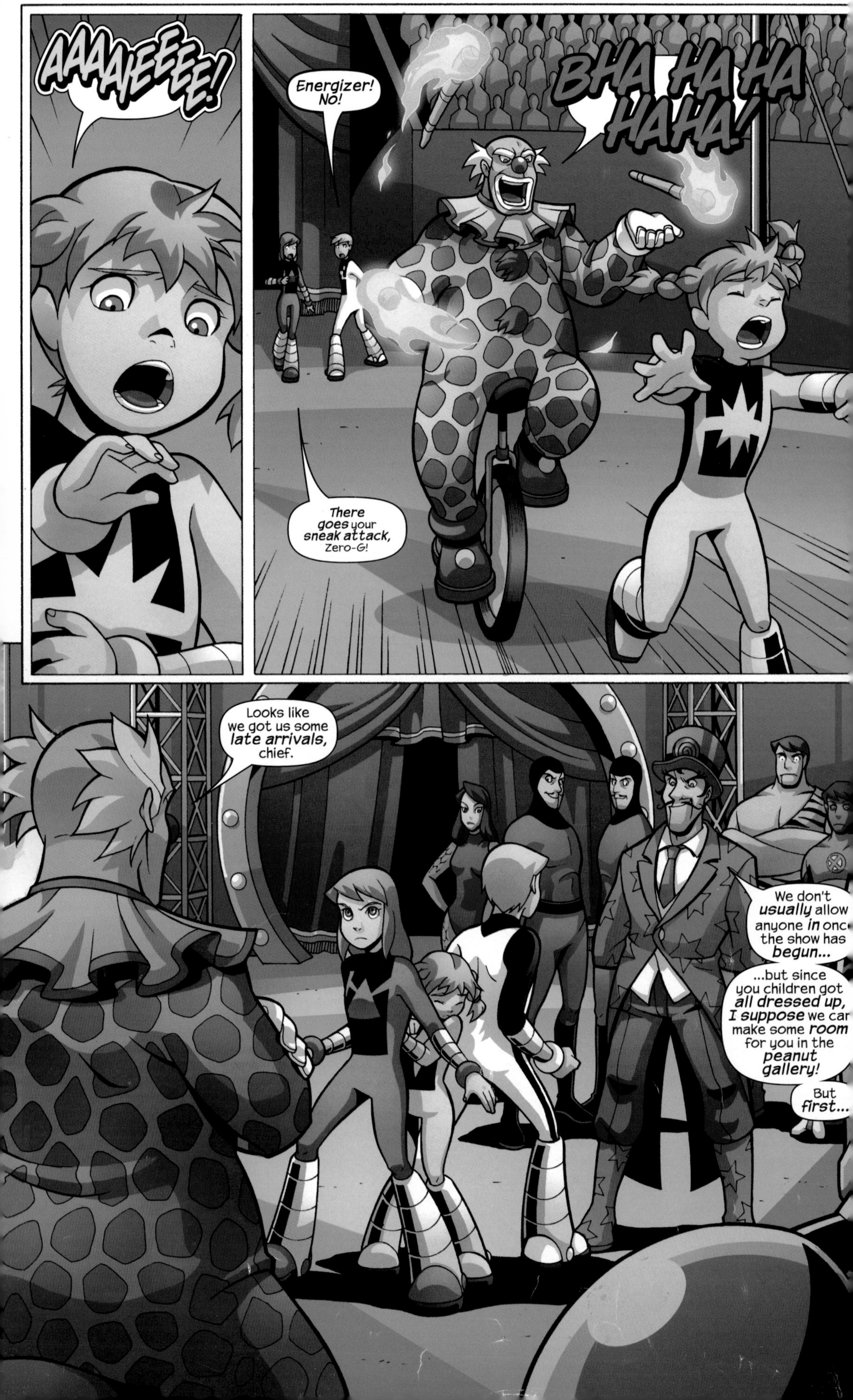
AAAAIEEEEE!
Energizer! NO!
BHA HA HA HAHA!
There goes your sneak attack, Zero-G!
Looks like we got us some late arrivals, chief.
We don't usually allow anyone in onc the show has begun...
...but since you children got all dressed up, I suppose we car make some room for you in the peanut gallery!
But first...

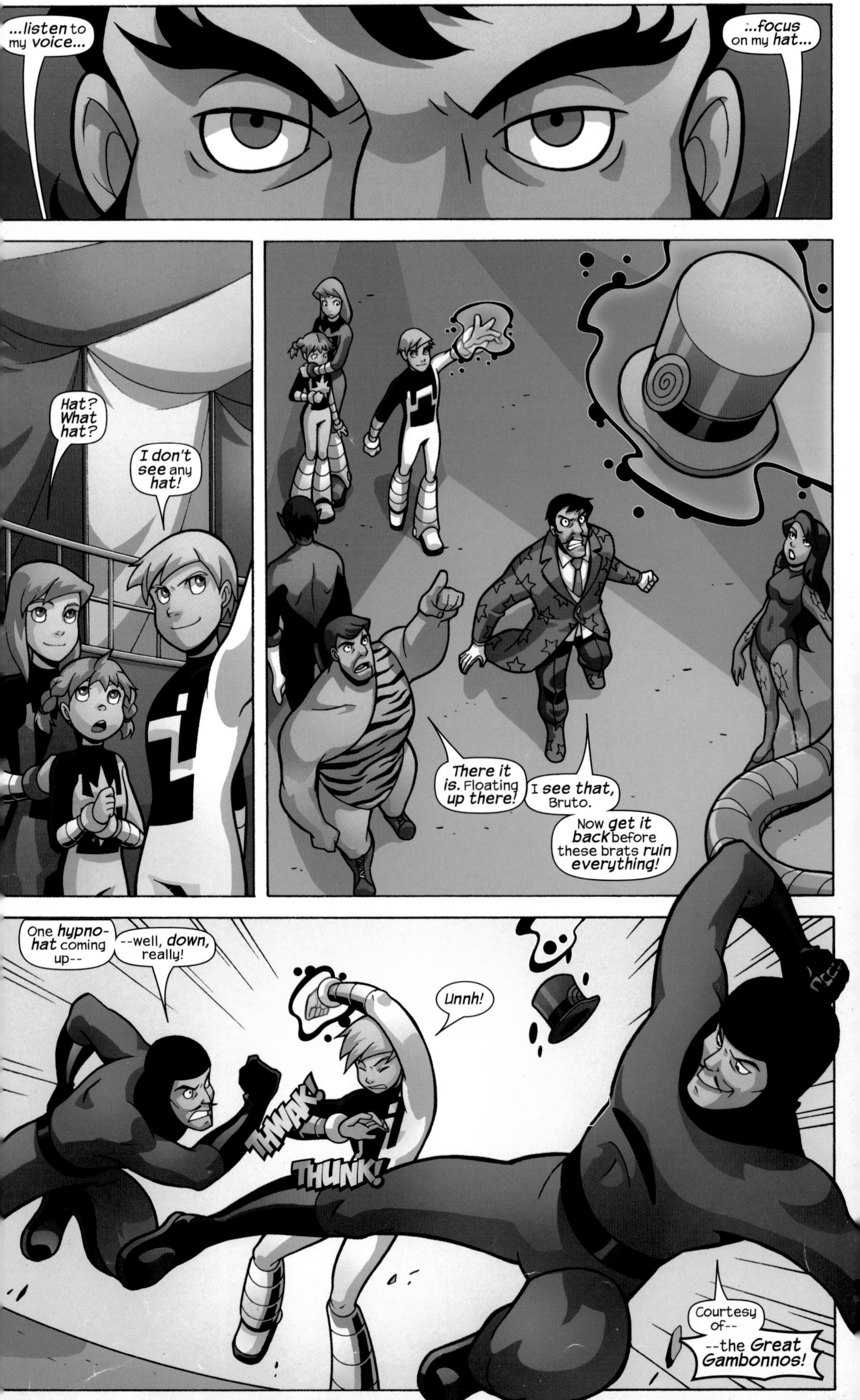
...listen to my voice...
...focus on my hat...
Hat? What hat?
I don't see any hat!
There it is. Floating up there!
I see that, Bruto.
Now get it back before these brats ruin everything!
One hypno-hat coming up--
--well, down, really!
Unnh!
THWAK!
THUNK!
Courtesy of--
--the Great Gambonnos!

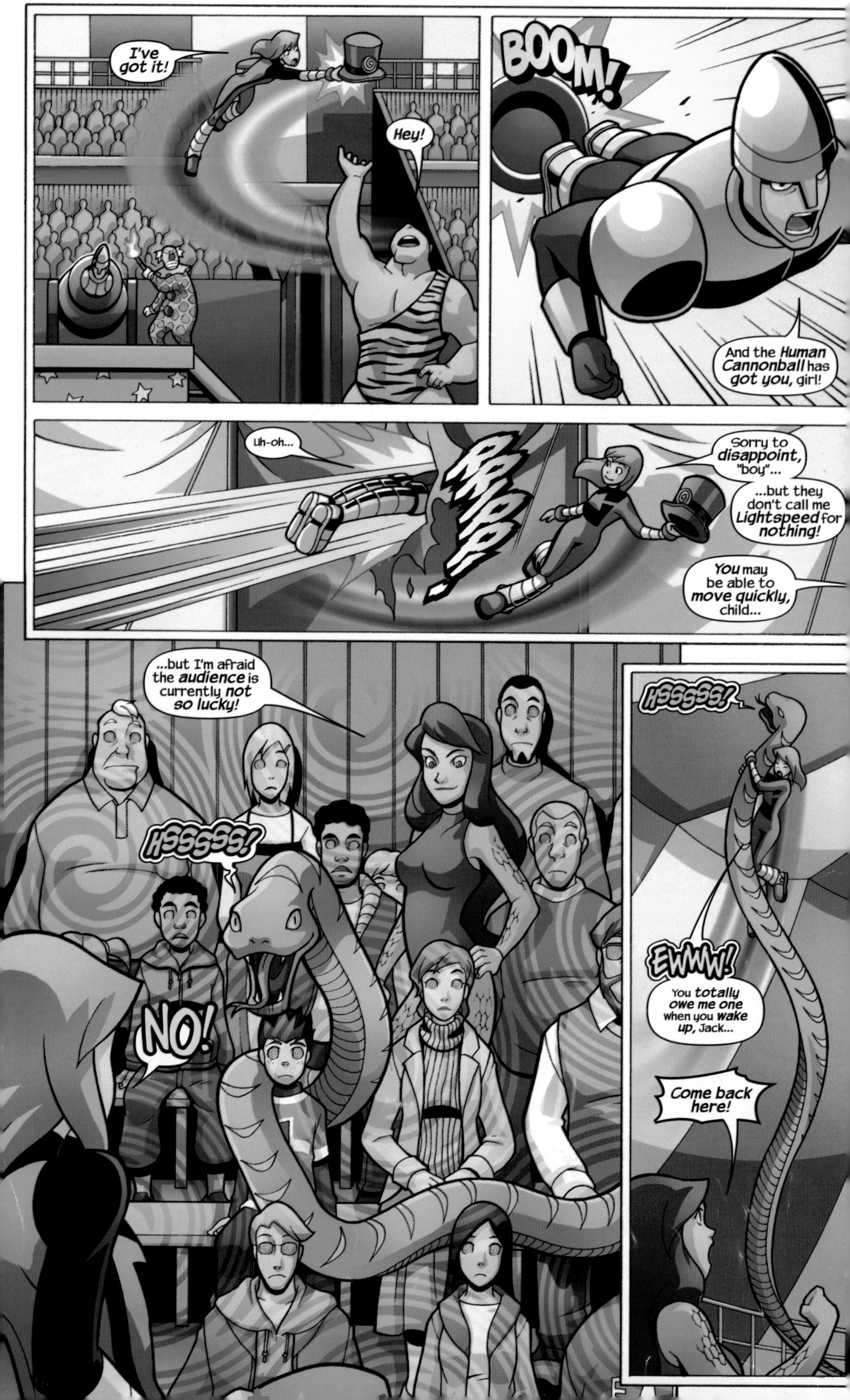
I've got it!
Hey!
BOOM!
And the Human Cannonball has got you, girl!
Uh-oh...
Sorry to disappoint, "boy"...
...but they don't call me Lightspeed for nothing!
You may be able to move quickly, child...
...but I'm afraid the audience is currently not so lucky!
HSSSSS!
NO!
HSSSSS!
EWWW!
You totally owe me one when you wake up, Jack...
Come back here!

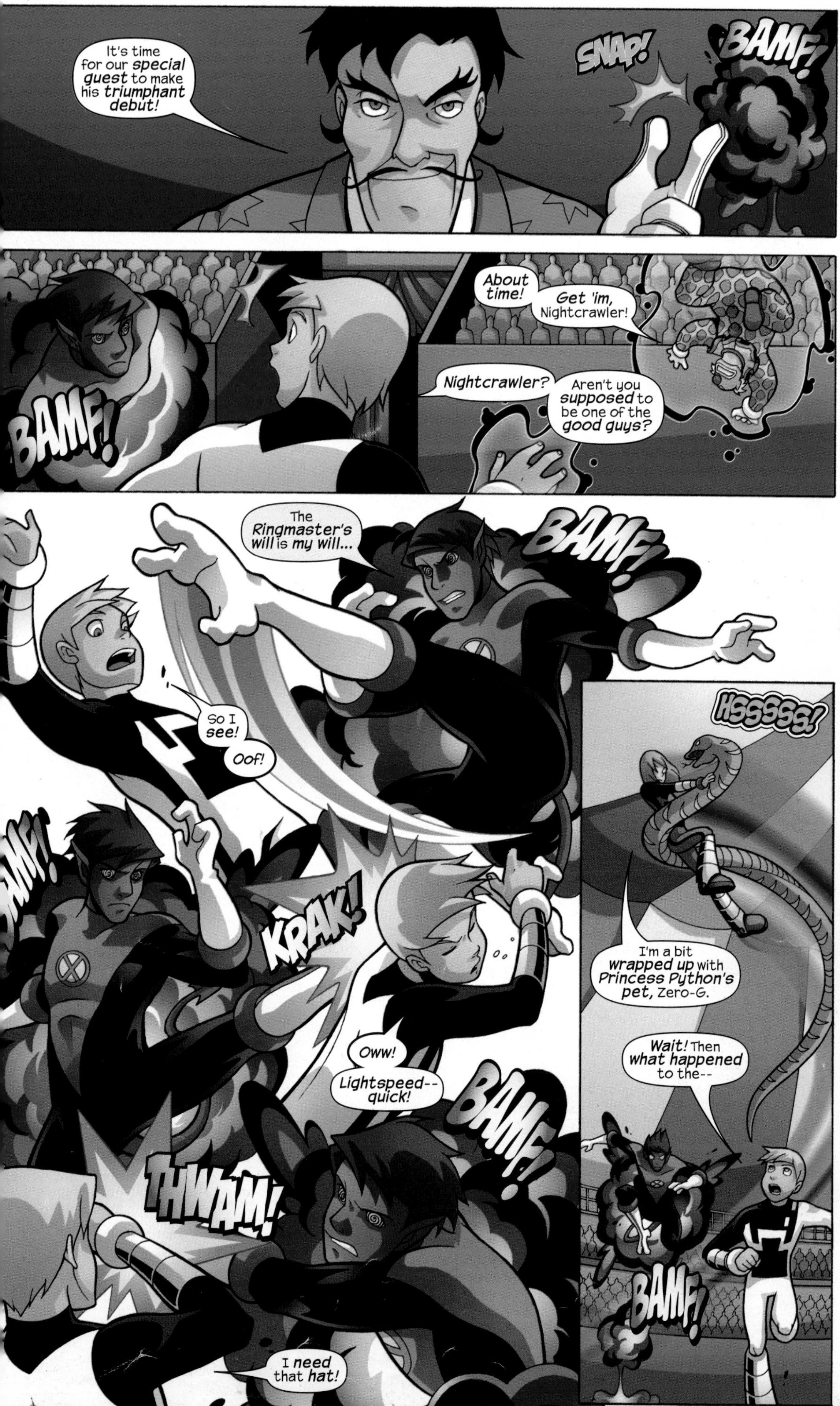
It's time for our special guest to make his triumphant debut!
SNAP!
BAMF!
BAMF!
About time!
Get 'im, Nightcrawler!
Nightcrawler?
Aren't you supposed to be one of the good guys?
The Ringmaster's will is my will...
BAMF!
So I see!
Oof!
HSSSSS!
KRAK!
I'm a bit wrapped up with Princess Python's pet, Zero-G.
Wait! Then what happened to the--
Oww!
Lightspeed--quick!
BAMF!
THWAM!
BAMF!
I need that hat!

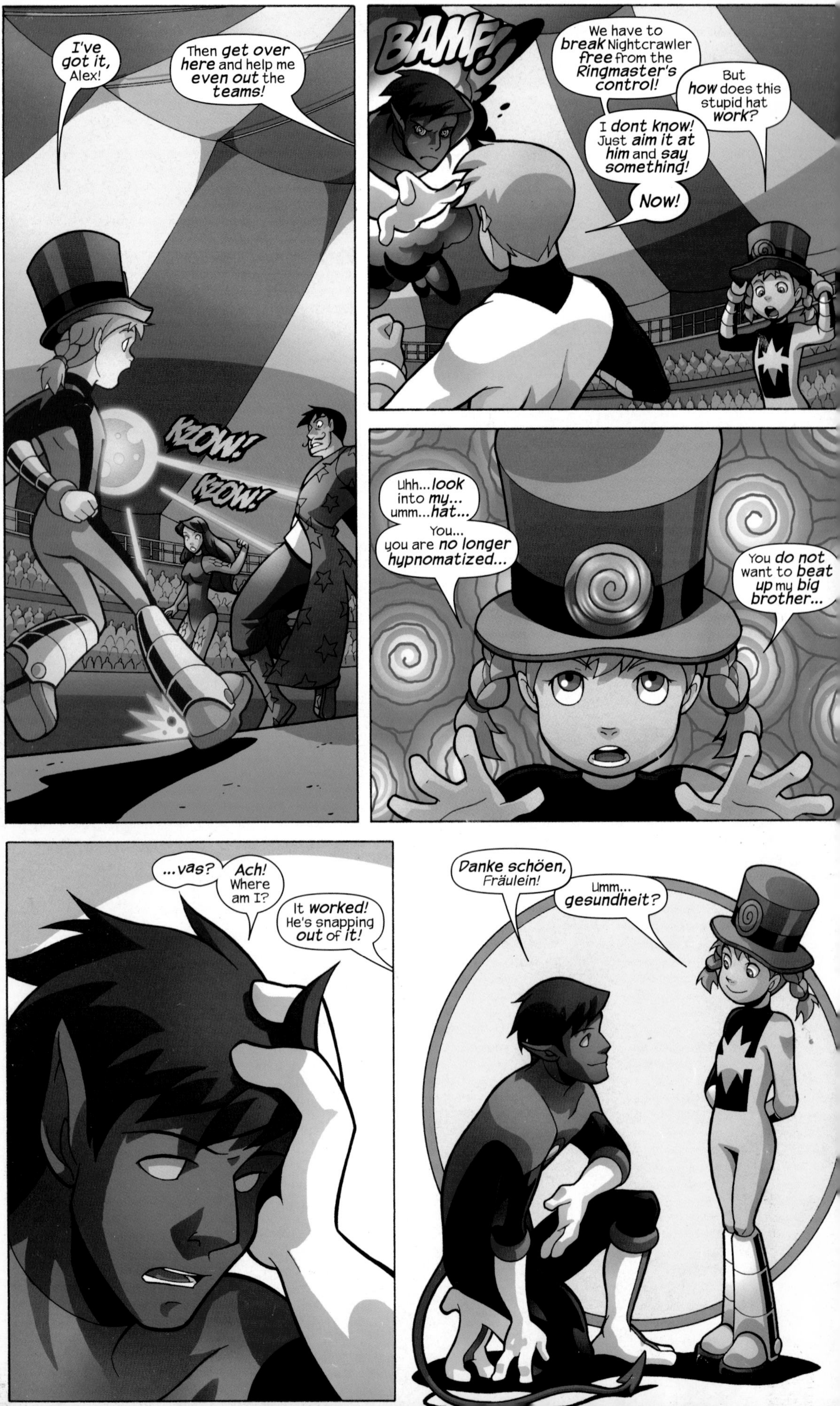
I've got it, Alex!
Then get over here and help me even out the teams!
KZOW!
KZOW!
BAMF!
We have to break Nightcrawler free from the Ringmaster's control!
But how does this stupid hat work?
I dont know! Just aim it at him and say something!
Now!
Uhh...look into my... umm...hat...
You... you are no longer hypnomatized...
You do not want to beat up my big brother...
...vas?
Ach! Where am I?
It worked! He's snapping out of it!
Danke schöen, Fräulein!
Umm... gesundheit?

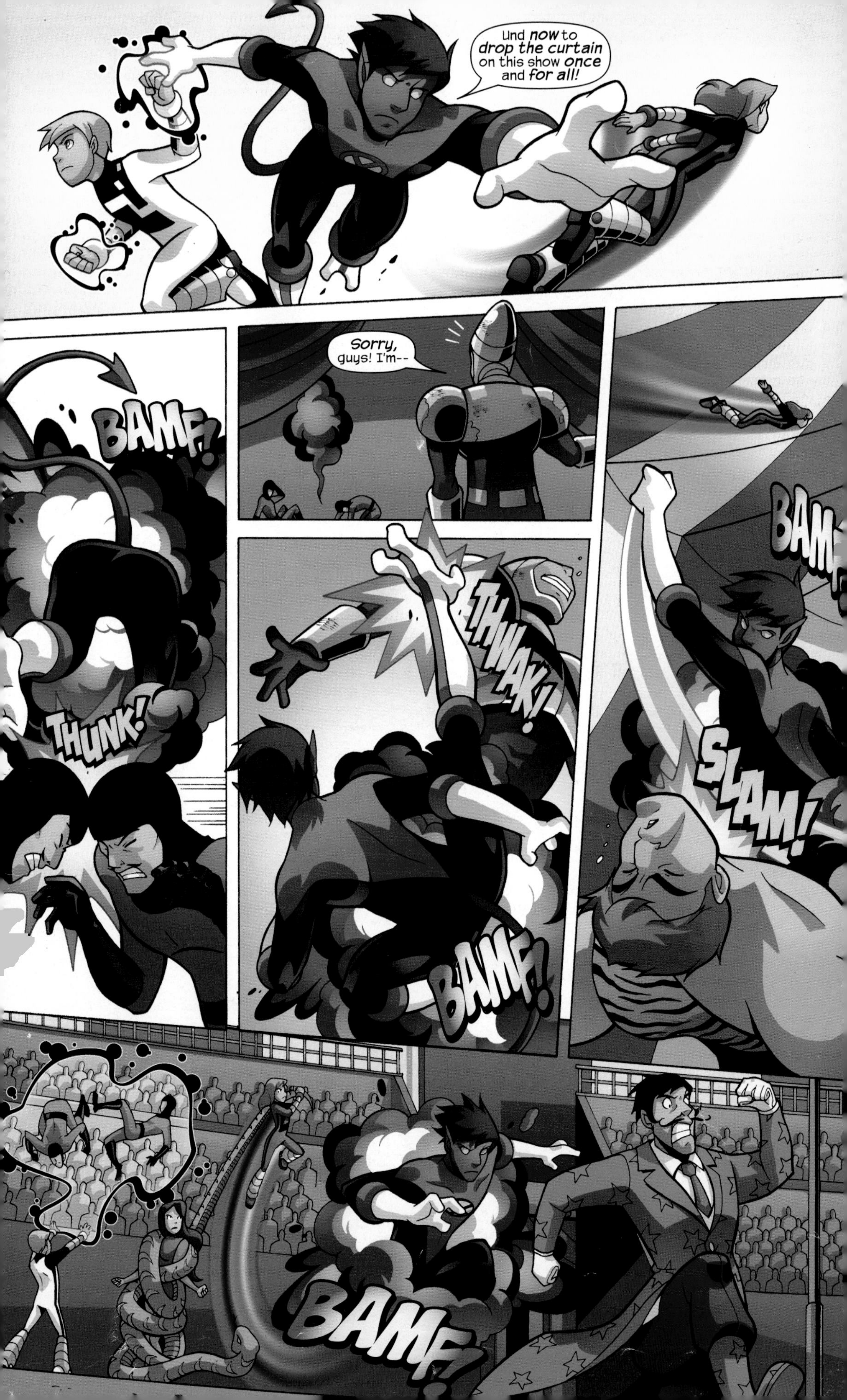
Und now to drop the curtain on this show once and for all!
BAMF!
THUNK!
Sorry, guys! I'm--
THWAK!
BAMF!
BAMF!
SLAM!
BAMF!

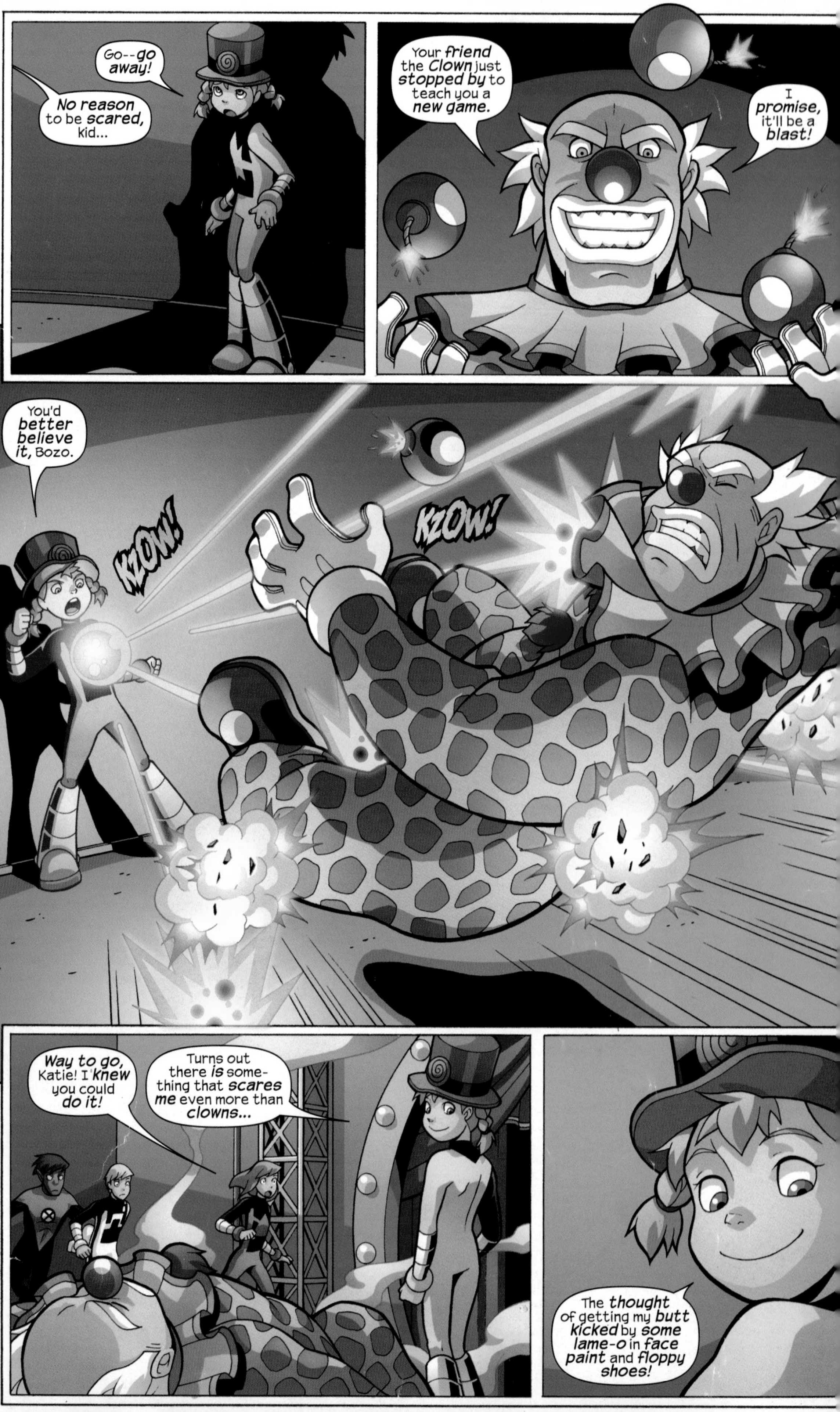
Go--go away!
No reason to be scared, kid...
Your friend the Clown just stopped by to teach you a new game.
I promise, it'll be a blast!
You'd better believe it, Bozo.
KZOW!
KZOW!
Way to go, Katie! I knew you could do it!
Turns out there is something that scares me even more than clowns...
The thought of getting my butt kicked by some lame-o in face paint and floppy shoes!

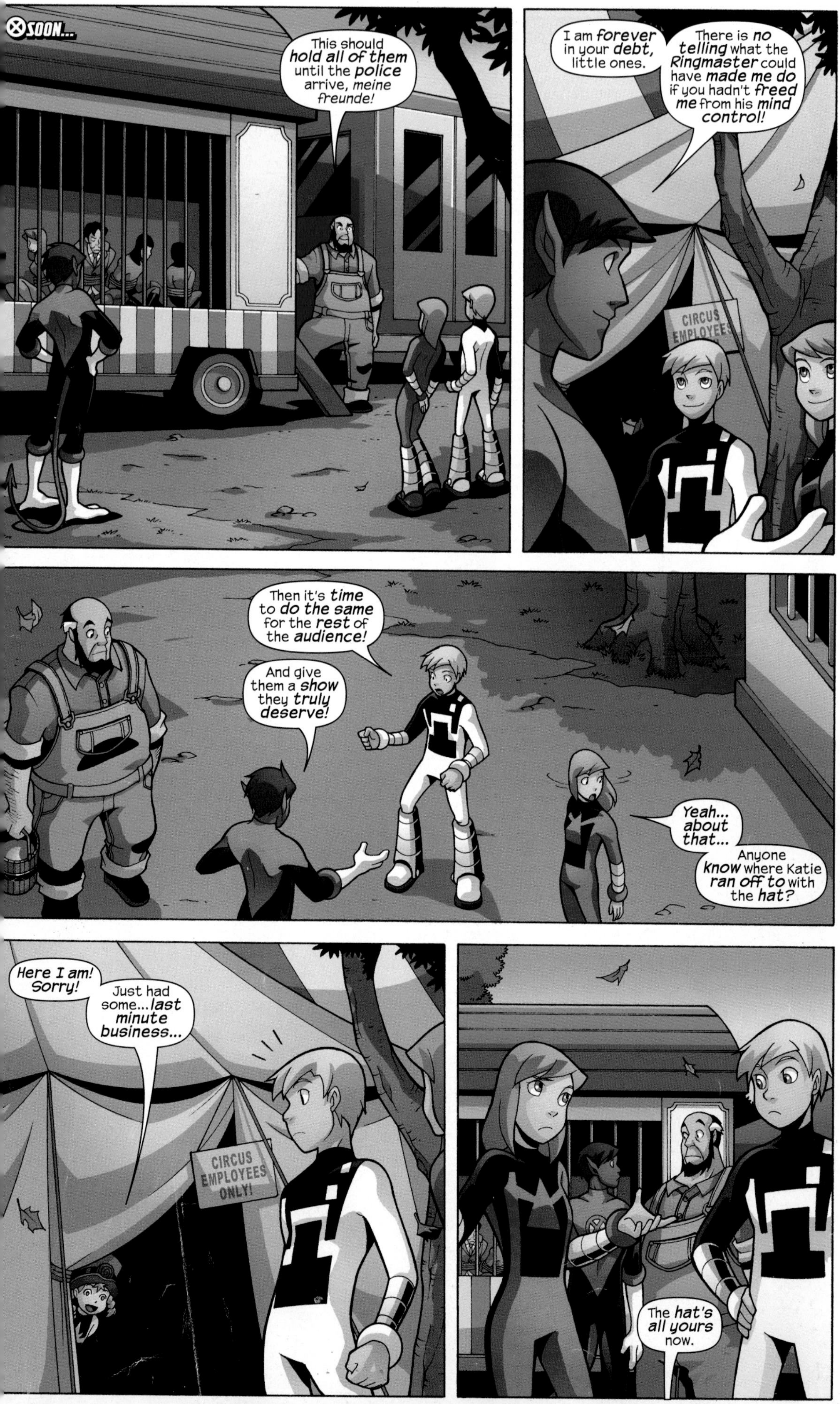
SOON...
This should hold all of them until the police arrive, meine freunde!
I am forever in your debt, little ones.
There is no telling what the Ringmaster could have made me do if you hadn't freed me from his mind control!
CIRCUS EMPLOYEES
Then it's time to do the same for the rest of the audience!
And give them a show they truly deserve!
Yeah... about that...
Anyone know where Katie ran off to with the hat?
Here I am! Sorry!
Just had some...last minute business...
CIRCUS EMPLOYEES ONLY!
The hat's all yours now.

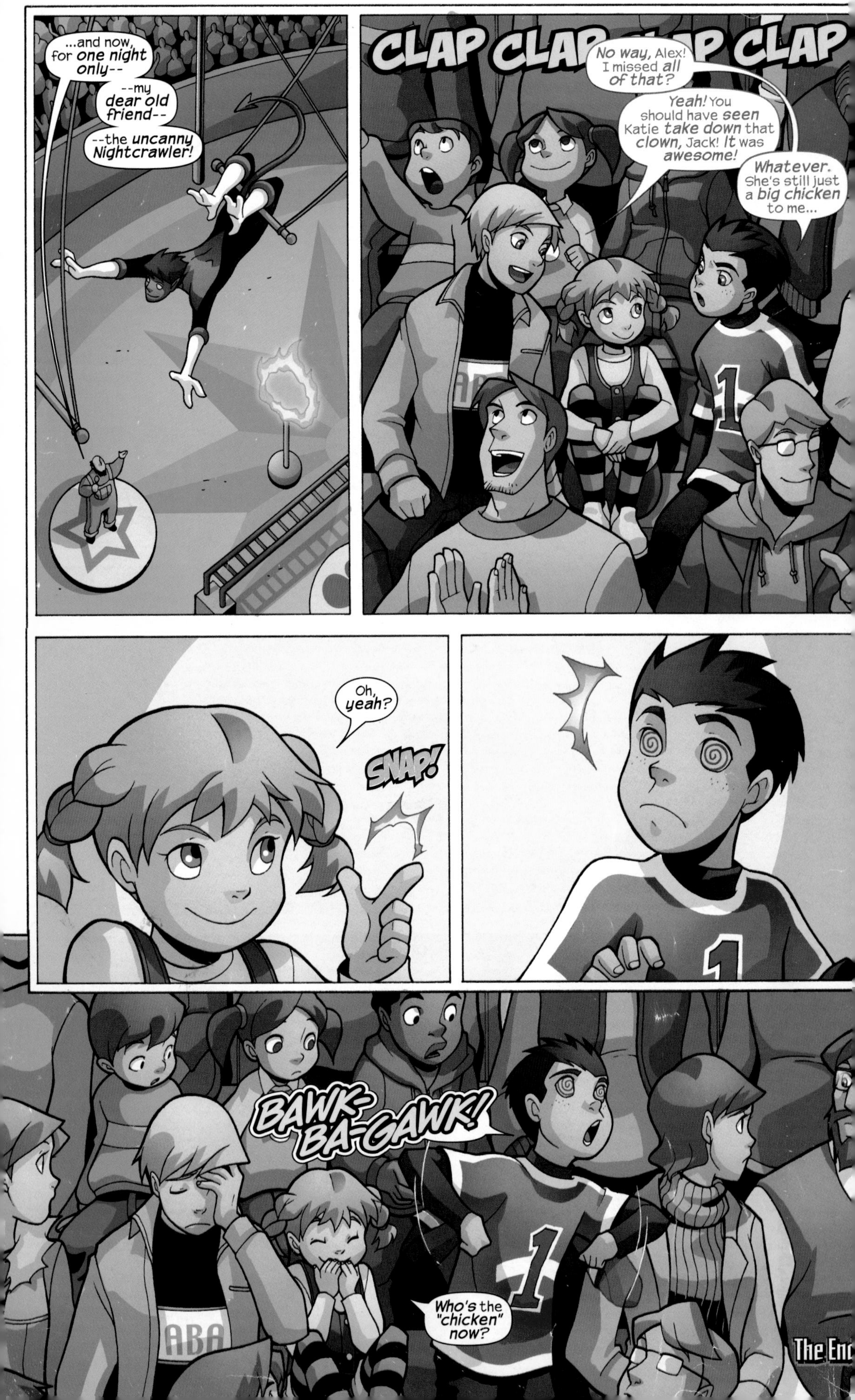
...and now, for one night only--
--my dear old friend--
--the uncanny Nightcrawler!
CLAP CLAP CLAP CLAP
No way, Alex! I missed all of that?
Yeah! You should have seen Katie take down that clown, Jack! It was awesome!
Whatever. She's still just a big chicken to me...
Oh, yeah?
SNAP!
BAWK-BA-GAWK!
Who's the "chicken" now?
The End